IF I LIVED ALONE

By Michaela Muntean
Illustrated by Carol Nicklaus

A SESAME STREET/READER'S DIGEST KIDS BOOK

Published by Reader's Digest Young Families, Inc.,
in cooperation with Children's Television Workshop

807102258

This is where I live.

My Mommy and Daddy live here.
My big sister Frieda and little brother Roger live here.

Sometimes it's noisy in my house.

Sometimes it's crowded in my house.

Sometimes I have to be quiet because Roger is asleep.

Sometimes I wish I lived alone.

If I lived alone, I could have a room all
to myself and everything in it would be
MINE! I could sit quietly all by myself, or I
could make as much noise as I wanted
whenever I wanted to.

But if I lived alone, I wouldn't have anyone to
talk to when it rains and thunders.

If I lived alone, I could eat chocolate ice cream for breakfast, vanilla ice cream for lunch, and strawberry ice cream for dinner. And I could eat as much as I wanted.

But if I lived alone, I wouldn't get to have any of Daddy's super-duper, flip-flop flapjacks.

If I lived alone, I wouldn't have to share my toys and books.

But if I lived alone, who would read to me?

If I lived alone, I could stay up as late as I wanted to.

But if I lived alone, who would hug me and kiss me
and tuck me in bed?

If I lived alone, I wouldn't have to pick up my toys or do anything I didn't want to do.

But if I lived alone, who would help me tie my shoelaces and who would put a bandage on my knee if I fell down?

If I lived alone, who would play baseball with Daddy?

Who would help him weed the garden?

If I lived alone, who would help Mommy with her sculpture?

Who would talk to her when she takes Roger for a walk?

If I lived alone, who would listen to Frieda's secrets?

Who would share Roger's crackers?

I guess I can't live alone—because if I lived alone, *everyone* would be lonely.